Smile, Lily!

For Lillian Grace, who always makes me smile —C. F.

For Auden and Sara Jane —Y. H.

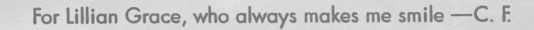

Atheneum Books for Young Readers
An imprint of Simon & Schuster Children's Publishing Division
1230 Avenue of the Americas, New York, New York 10020
Text copyright © 2004 by Candace Fleming
Illustrations copyright © 2004 by Yumi Heo
Book design by Polly Kanevsky
The text for this book is set in Graham.
The illustrations for this book are
rendered in oils, pencil, and collage.
Manufactured in China
First Edition
10 9 8 7 6 5 4 3 2 1
Library of Congress
Cataloging-in-Publication Data
Smile, Lily!
by Candace Fleming.—1st ed.
p. cm.
Summary: Family members try everything
to stop the baby Lily from crying.
ISBN 0-689-83548-5
[1. Babies—Fiction.] I. Title.
PZ7.F59936 Sm 2001
[E]—dc21
99-088933

Smile, Lily!

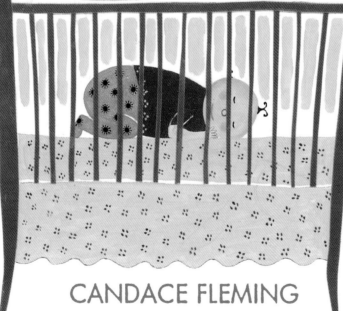

CANDACE FLEMING
illustrated by YUMI HEO

An Anne Schwartz Book
Atheneum Books for Young Readers
New York · London · Toronto · Sydney · Singapore

Lily wakes up crying.

Waa! Waa! Waa!

Lily wakes up crying.
Oh, who knows what to do?

"I do",
says Lily's mommy.

She sings a lullaby.
She hums of far-off places.
She hums of starry skies.
She presses Lily to her heart
and rocks her in a chair.
"Husha. Husha," Mommy croons.
"There. There. There."

But Lily keeps on crying.

Waa!
Waa!
Waa!

Lily keeps
on crying.
Oh, who knows
what to do?

"I do",  says Lily's daddy.

He takes her in his arms.
He swings her gently left and right.
He swings her all around.
He tickles Lily's tummy,
and he holds her way up high.
"Superbaby!"
Daddy whoops.
"Fly! Fly! Fly!"

But Lily keeps on crying.

Waa! Waa! Waa!

Lily keeps on crying.
Oh, who knows what to do?

She lays Lily on her back.
She unsnaps Lily's T-shirt.
She unsnaps Lily's pants.
She powders Lily's bottom,
and she nibbles Lily's feet.
"You smell delicious,"
Grandma sighs.
"Sweet. Sweet. Sweet."

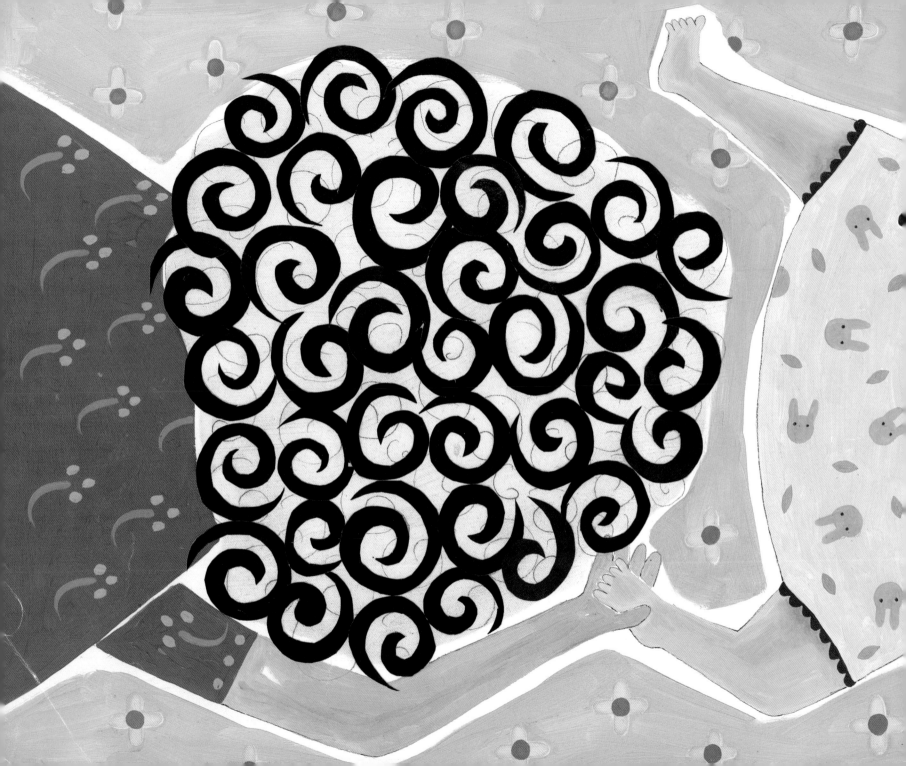

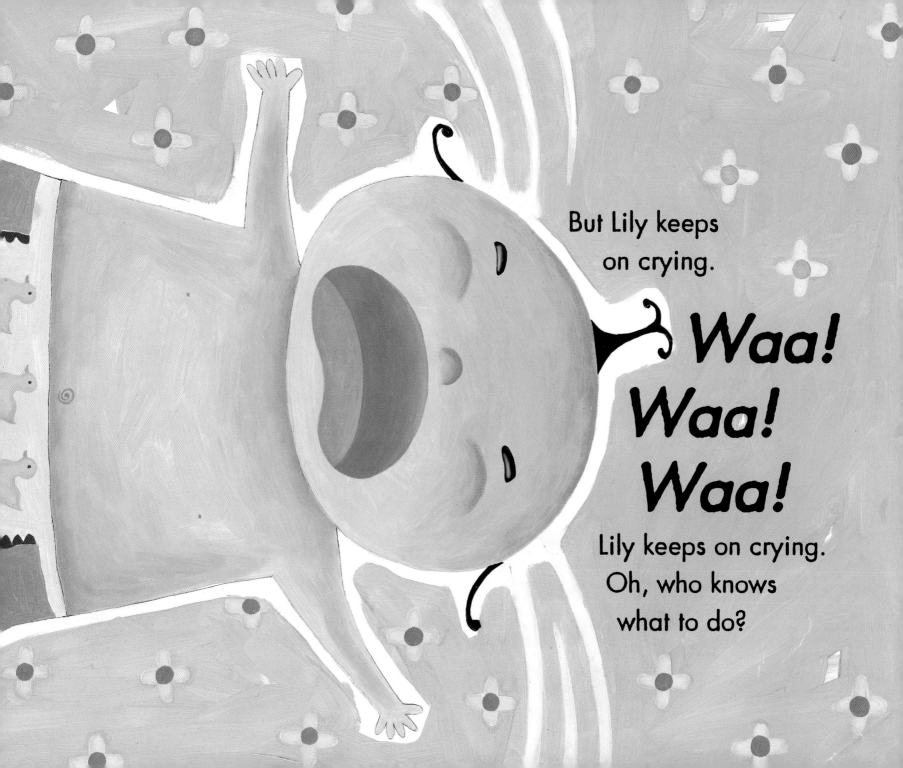

But Lily keeps
on crying.

**Waa!
Waa!
Waa!**

Lily keeps on crying.
Oh, who knows
what to do?

"I do", says Lily's grandpa.

He sits Lily in her chair.
He spoons a bite of oatmeal.
He spoons a bite of pear.
He chugs the spoon toward Lily's mouth,
makes silly noises too.
"Here's the choo-choo!"

Grandpa says.
"Woo! Woo! Woo!"

But Lily keeps on crying.

Waa! Waa! Waa!

Lily keeps on crying.
Oh, who knows what to do?

"I do,"
says Lily's uncle.

He rides Lily on his knee.
He shakes her favorite rattle.
He shakes her plastic keys.
He hides his face behind his hands
and pops out—

Waa!
Waa!
Waa!

Lily keeps
on crying.
No one knows
what to do!

"Call the doctor!" Mommy panics.
Daddy grabs the phone.
Grandma says a little prayer.
Grandpa starts to groan.
Uncle paces up and down,

so Brother grabs his chance.

He tiptoes to his sister. He knows JUST what to do.

And with everybody smiling,
Lily smiles too!